GUS and GRANDPA
and the Two-Wheeled Bike

Claudia Mills ★ Pictures by Catherine Stock

SQUARE
FISH

Farrar Straus Giroux
New York

To Catherine Stock
— C.M.

For Claudia, the front wheel
— C.S.

**SQUARE·
FISH**

An Imprint of Macmillan
175 Fifth Avenue
New York, NY 10010
mackids.com

Library of Congress Cataloging-in-Publication Data
Mills, Claudia.
Gus and Grandpa and the two-wheeled bike/ Claudia Mills ; pictures by Catherine Stock
p. cm.
Summary: Gus doesn't want to give up the training wheels on his bike, even for a new five-
speed bicycle, until Grandpa helps him learn to get along without them.
ISBN 978-0-374-42816-7
[1. Bicycles and bicycling—Fiction. 2. Grandfathers—Fiction.]
I. Stock, Catherine, ill. II. Title.

PZ7.M63963Gude   1999   [E]—dc21   97-44203

Originally published in the United States by Farrar Straus Giroux
First Square Fish Edition: 2013
Square Fish logo designed by Filomena Tuosto

7   9   10   8

AR: 2.9 / LEXILE: 430L

Contents

Training Wheels

Gus was the only kid
on Maple Street
who still had training wheels
on his bike.
Gus didn't mind.
He liked training wheels.
With training wheels,
his bike didn't tip.
The wheels didn't wobble.
His bike didn't fall over.
It was easy to ride
a bike with training wheels.
Why would anybody
not want training wheels?

Ryan Mason lived next door.
Ryan was the same age as Gus.
But his bike had
no training wheels.
His bike had five speeds,
and hand brakes,
and a special holder
for a water bottle.

"Look at me!"
Ryan called to Gus
one evening
when the two boys
were out riding their bikes
up and down the street.

"Watch me stop
with my hand brakes!"

Gus stopped with his foot brakes.

Ryan coasted
to a smooth stop.
"What gear do you think
I should be in?"
he asked Gus.

Gus didn't know.
He wasn't sure what a gear was,
exactly.

Ryan took a long drink
from his water bottle.
He didn't offer any water
to Gus.

"How come you still ride
with training wheels?"
Ryan asked Gus.

"I like training wheels,"
Gus said.

Gus's father was watching.
He said,
"Gus, do you want me
to take off
those training wheels?"

"No," Gus said.
He couldn't ride a tippy,
slippy,
floppy,
falling-over bike
without training wheels.

"Let's just try
taking them off,"
Gus's father said.

"No!" Gus told him.
He kept on pedaling.

The New Bike

The next day, Gus's grandpa
came over to visit.
Gus and Grandpa
were playing rummy
in the kitchen when they heard
Gus's father call to them.

"Gus! Dad!
Come into the garage!
I have a surprise for you!"

Gus and Grandpa
grinned at each other.
They liked surprises.

In the garage,
Gus's mother and father
were standing next to
a brand-new bike.
It was as bright and shiny
as Ryan Mason's.
It had five speeds,
and hand brakes,
and a special holder
for a water bottle.
It had no training wheels.

Gus stared at the bike.
He liked the water bottle.
He could imagine himself
on a hot day,
taking long sips of cool water
straight from the bottle,
the way Ryan Mason did.

"Pretty fancy,"
Grandpa said.

"Let's give it a whirl,"
Gus's father said.

Gus's mouth felt dry.
He took a sip of water
from his new water bottle.
His mouth still felt dry.
He would never be able to ride
this fancy new bike.
But he had to try.

Daddy held the bike for him.

Gus climbed on.

The bike felt tippy.

It felt slippy.

Daddy started explaining
about the gears.
Gus didn't understand
what he was saying.

The new bike was taller
than Gus's old bike.
The wheels were wobblier.
The ground looked far away.

Gus started to pedal slowly
while his father held on
to the back of the bike.
Then his father let go
for just a second.
The new bike crashed.
Gus crashed, too.

The Old, Old Bike

A few days
and a few crashes later,
Gus went to visit Grandpa
at Grandpa's house.
Grandpa's dog, Skipper,
jumped up to lick him.
Skipper didn't mind
that Gus still rode a bike
with training wheels.

Gus and Skipper
ran around Grandpa's yard
until they were both panting.

Then Gus sat down
next to Grandpa
and drank some of Grandpa's
homemade root beer.
It tasted even better
than water from the water bottle.

"How's the bike riding
coming along?"
Grandpa asked.

"I can't ride that new bike,"
Gus said.
"It keeps on crashing."
He pointed to his knees.
He had a dinosaur Band-Aid
on the right knee.
He had a monster Band-Aid
on the left knee.

"I have an idea,"
Grandpa said.

Grandpa led the way
to his broken-down shed.
Gus and Skipper followed.
Gus loved Grandpa's shed.
It was filled with junk.

"Let's look in here,"
Grandpa said.

"I think I still have
your daddy's old bike,
the one he had when
he was a little boy."

Grandpa pushed aside
a cracked door
with peeling paint.
He looked behind
a bunch of boxes.
"Here it is,"
he finally said.

The bike looked like
Gus's old bike,
but even older.
This was an *old*, old bike.
Its red paint was rusty.
Its tires were flat.
"We'll fix it up,"
Grandpa said.

Gus suddenly felt hopeful.
His daddy had learned how
to ride this bike long ago.
Maybe he could learn how
to ride it now.

No Training Wheels

When the old, old bike
was ready,
Grandpa loaded it
into the back of his car.
Gus and Grandpa and Skipper
drove to an empty parking lot
on the other side
of the railroad tracks
near Grandpa's house.

"Once you learn to ride a bike,"
Grandpa told Gus,
"you never forget.
Sometimes I can't remember
what I ate for breakfast,
but I always remember
how to ride a bike."

Grandpa got on the old, old bike.
He rode it once
around the parking lot.
Skipper barked.
Gus laughed.
Grandpa looked funny
riding such a little bike.

"Now it's your turn,"
Grandpa said.
He held the bike
while Gus climbed on.
Gus started pedaling.
Grandpa ran behind him,
holding the back of the bike.

Gus rode
around the parking lot
with Grandpa
a million times.
They stopped
so that Grandpa could rest.

Then Gus rode
around the parking lot
with Grandpa
a million more times.
And a million more.

Suddenly Gus felt the bike
begin to tip.
"You can do it!"
Grandpa said.
Gus pedaled faster.
The bike didn't fall over.

Gus kept on pedaling.
The bike rode so smoothly
that Gus felt
as if he were flying.
When Gus turned around a curve,
his bike turned with him,
like a winged horse
galloping across the sky.

Then Gus saw Grandpa
standing beside the car
with Skipper,
waving to him!
Gus flashed Grandpa
a big smile
and pedaled on.

Gus wished Ryan Mason
could see him now.
There was nothing in the world
as wonderful as
riding a bike
without training wheels.
Gus knew Grandpa was right.
He would never ever
forget how to ride a bike.

And he would never
forget that Grandpa
had taught him how.
He would remember that forever.